Penake

They Are Searching
for a Pink Brontosaurus.
You and Your Friends
Have Him.

All day long you play with Harvey. Every time you hear a helicopter, you cover him up with sand. Nobody except you and your friends knows where Harvey is.

But soon it is time to go home. Harvey loves the park so much that he refuses to leave.

You are afraid that he will be captured during the night.

If you try to put Harvey on wheels and roll him home, turn to page 42.

If you disguise Harvey as a tree, turn to page 44.

If you decide that Harvey really belongs in the zoo, turn to page 54.

WHAT WILL HAPPEN NEXT?

WHICH WAY SECRET DOOR Books for you to enjoy

Available from ARCHWAY paperbacks

which way · secret door · books

#10

R.G. Austin

Brontosaurus Moves In

Illustrated by
Joseph A. Smith

AN ARCHWAY PAPERBACK
Published by POCKET BOOKS • NEW YORK

AN ARCHWAY PAPERBACK *Original*

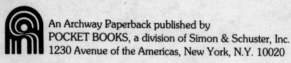

An Archway Paperback published by
POCKET BOOKS, a division of Simon & Schuster, Inc.
1230 Avenue of the Americas, New York, N.Y. 10020

ISBN: 0-671-47571-1

First Archway Paperback printing January, 1984

10 9 8 7 6 5 4 3 2 1

AN ARCHWAY PAPERBACK and colophon are
trademarks of Simon & Schuster, Inc.

WHICH WAY is a registered trademark
of Simon & Schuster, Inc.

SECRET DOOR is a trademark
of Simon & Schuster, Inc.

Printed in the U.S.A.

II   1+

For Katie

ATTENTION!

READING A SECRET DOOR BOOK
IS LIKE PLAYING A GAME.

HERE ARE THE RULES

Begin reading on page 1. When you come to a choice, decide what to do and follow the directions. Keep reading and following the directions until you come to an ending. Then go back to the beginning and make new choices.

There are many stories and many endings in this book.

HAVE FUN!

It is dark outside. You have gone to bed, but you are still wide awake.

You lie quietly until everyone in the house is asleep. Then you creep out of bed and tiptoe into the closet.

You push away the clothes and knock three times on the back wall. Soon the secret door begins to move. It opens just wide enough for you to slip through.

Turn to page 2.

What a disappointment! You are in your very own living room. You wanted an adventure, and now all you have is the same old thing.

You turn on the TV.

The program is just getting started when the doorbell rings. You open the door. Standing right in front of you is a pink brontosaurus!

If you invite the brontosaurus in, turn to page 4.

If you go outside to play with the brontosaurus, turn to page 6.

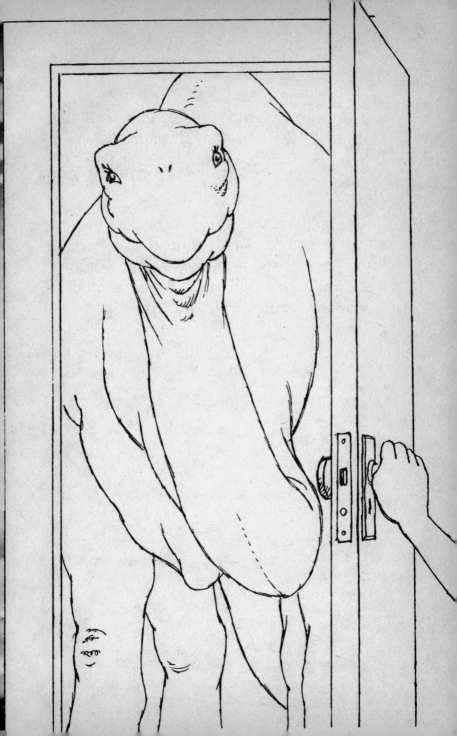

The brontosaurus is so big that you have to push and shove him through the door. When he is inside, he licks your face.

He's nice! you think. *I think I'll call him Harvey.*

Then Harvey sticks his head into the kitchen. You feed him a head of lettuce, a bunch of carrots, six tomatoes, nine onions, a stalk of celery, and three dozen potatoes.

Harvey nuzzles your neck to say thank you.

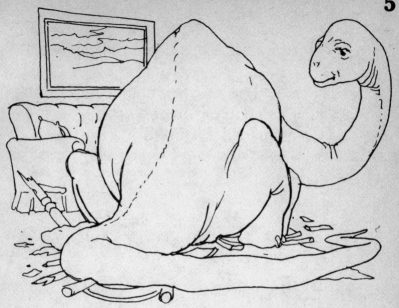

Then Harvey sits down on the sofa. CRASH!

He sits on a chair. CRUNCH!

When he gets up, he pokes a hole in the ceiling.

This dinosaur may be gentle, you think, but he sure is trouble. I better get him out of here!

Just then you hear a news bulletin on TV.

Turn to page 12.

You run outside. You cannot believe your luck!

"Hooray! I have a new pet," you shout. "I think I'll name him Harvey."

Then you make a leash for Harvey and head for the park.

*If you take Harvey to the playground,
turn to page 8.*

*If you take him to the swimming pool,
turn to page 10.*

You take Harvey to the playground. The children think he is the greatest toy that they have ever seen.

They feed him grass. They feed him leaves. They crawl all over him.

Everybody is happy. Even Harvey.

Then you hear a helicopter.

"Uh-oh," you say. "They're coming to get Harvey."

"What will we do?" the children shout. "We can't let them take Harvey away."

You look up. The helicopter is lowering a huge net.

If you try to destroy the net, turn to page 34.

If you try to protect Harvey, turn to page 36.

"You can't take that brontosaurus into the pool!" the lifeguard yells. He blows his whistle.

But it is too late. Harvey jumps in.

"Help!" cry the grown-ups.

"Hooray!" shout the children.

Then you hear a siren! A police car pulls up. Two policemen walk right over to you.

"I'm sorry," a policeman says, "but I am going to give you a ticket for . . . for . . . I don't know . . ."

The policeman scratches his head. Then he looks at his friend. "Is there a law against dinosaurs being in swimming pools?"

"No, sir," says the other policeman.

"Well then, no ticket. But I want that monster out of the pool right this minute!"

If you try to get Harvey out of the pool by tempting him with a hamburger, turn to page 46.

If you ask the policeman to let the brontosaurus stay in the pool until you figure out what to do with Harvey, turn to page 48.

"A pink brontosaurus has been seen roaming the streets," the announcer says. "If you see him, call the zoo immediately. Be careful. He may be dangerous!"

Harvey's not dangerous! you think. *But he is a problem. If I keep him here, he'll destroy the house. If I let him out, he'll be captured and put in a cage.*

You decide that you will have to hide Harvey.

If you call your friend, Steven, to help you take Harvey to the lake, turn to page 14.

If you take Harvey to the museum so he can hide among the other dinosaurs, turn to page 16.

"It's lucky that the lake is so close by," you tell Steven as you push Harvey back out the door.

"Come on, Harvey!" you say. "Hurry!"

In no time, you get to the lake. But Harvey won't go into the water.

Just then, you hear a helicopter.
"What are we going to do?" Steven asks.
"They must be looking for Harvey!"

If you try to push Harvey into the lake, turn to page 18.

If you try to hide Harvey in the trees, turn to page 20.

You tie a long rope around Harvey's neck and you lead him to the museum. You take the path through the woods so that nobody will see you.

Then you sneak in the back door of the museum.

All of a sudden, you hear voices.

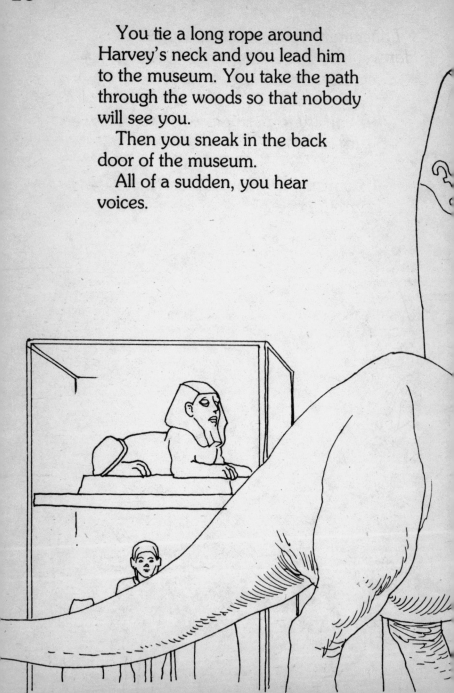

I have to hide him! you think. *If they catch Harvey, they'll take him away!*

If you try to hide Harvey in the closet, turn to page 30.

If you walk Harvey to the dinosaur exhibit, turn to page 32.

The two of you push and shove. And shove and push. And push and shove.

Finally, Harvey walks into the lake.

The water is very dirty from moss and algae and green slime. Harvey walks deeper and deeper into the yucky water.

"He's disappeared!" Steven says with tears in his eyes. "He's going to drown!"

Soon the helicopter flies over. There is no sign of Harvey.

When the helicopter leaves, Harvey walks out of the water.

"Look!" you say. "He has a breathing hole on the top of his head. His head was under the water, but his breathing hole was out!"

Harvey is covered with green slime. He is munching away on moss and algae.

"Look!" you say. "He likes the guck. He's eating it! Pretty soon he'll clean up the whole lake. Everyone will love Harvey when they see what he can do! They'll never put him in a cage!"

Harvey is saved!

The End

You and Steven walk Harvey into the trees. Then you realize that the helicopters will be able to see the pink dinosaur through the branches.

"We have to camouflage him," you say.

If you tell Steven to help gather some branches so that you can put them on top of Harvey, turn to page 22.

If you tell Steven to run into town and buy some paint, turn to page 24.

You pile branches on top of Harvey. But every time you put a branch on him, he turns and eats the leaves!

"He's eating our camouflage!" you say.

You pile on even more branches. Harvey eats them, too—or he knocks them off his back.

"I hear a helicopter!" Steven yells. "It's almost here!"

You and Steven work very hard. But you cannot cover poor Harvey.

The helicopter begins to land.

"Oh, no," you say. You begin to cry. "Here they come, and they're going to lock Harvey up in a cage!"

Turn to page 26.

Steven runs to the hardware store. Soon he is back with jars of green and brown poster paint. He hands you one of the brushes.

You and Steven start to paint a camouflage pattern all over the brontosaurus.

Harvey begins to move. Then he begins to wiggle. Then he begins to shake.

"I don't think Harvey likes getting painted," you say.

"I don't think so either," Steven says.

But you both keep on painting.

You have just finished when you hear someone yelling.

"Help!" cries a voice. "Help! I can't swim!"

Turn to page 28.

The helicopter lands. Three men climb out and walk toward you. One of them is carrying a gun with a big dart in it.

"Don't shoot!" you say. "This is a gentle dinosaur."

"It's only a tranquilizer gun," the man says. "It will put him to sleep."

"Please wait!" you say. "Let me tell you about Harvey!"

You explain to the men about how wonderful Harvey is. And you tell them that you are sure he would be miserable in a cage in the zoo. Then you suggest that Harvey would be very happy in the jungle.

"Well, I guess we could fly him to the jungle," one of them suggests.

"Yeah, I guess we could," says another.

And that is exactly what happens. You are sure that Harvey is happy there with all those leaves to eat.

The End

You and Steven run to the lake. A little girl has fallen into the water.

"I'm not a good enough swimmer to save her. Are you?" Steven asks.

"No. What will we do?"

Just then Harvey walks over. When he sees the little girl in the water, he stretches out his long, long neck and grabs the girl by her dress.

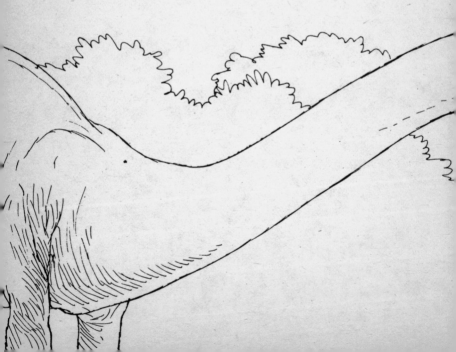

Then he lifts her out of the water.

"You saved her! You saved her!" you yell.

Just then, you notice a helicopter over-head. Soon it lands next to you.

"What are we going to do?" Steven asks. "They will take him away."

"Nobody is going to lock up a hero," you say. "And Harvey is the *biggest* hero any-body has ever seen!"

The End

You open the door to the closet and try to shove Harvey inside. Even though it is a very big closet, it is not big enough for Harvey!

The voices grow louder. Then a man and a woman walk around the corner.

"Look!" the woman yells. "It's the dinosaur!"

"Please," you beg, with tears in your eyes. "Please don't take him to the zoo."

"Take him to the zoo?" the man says. "Don't be silly. We want to give him a home here. He can live in that big field behind the museum. He'll be the greatest exhibit in the world! We'll all be famous."

And then he adds, "And so will you."

The End

You walk Harvey through the museum and into the dinosaur exhibit. Luckily, nobody sees you.

In the Hall of Dinosaurs there are models of dinosaurs, and there are huge skeletons.

Harvey is so glad to see the dinosaurs that he wags his tail.

CRASH! BAM!

"There's the dinosaur!" says one of the museum guards. "Catch him! Get him out of here! Put him in a cage!"

"No, stop!" says a man. "I'm a Hollywood producer. I'll take the dinosaur home with me, and I'll make him a movie star. He can live on my ranch in California."

"May I come visit him?" you ask.

"Sure," says the producer. "I'll put you in the movies too."

The End

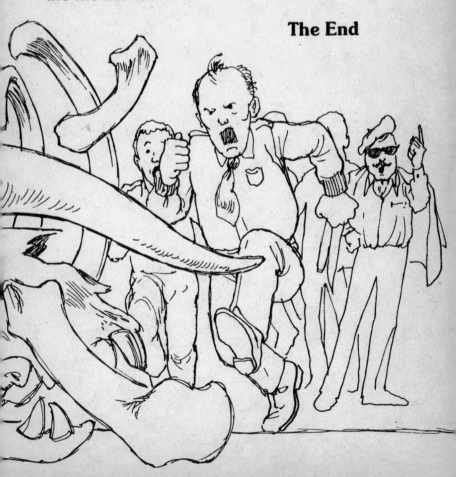

You tell the kids to run to the arts and crafts booth and bring back scissors.

As soon as the net is lowered, everyone cuts the strings in the net.

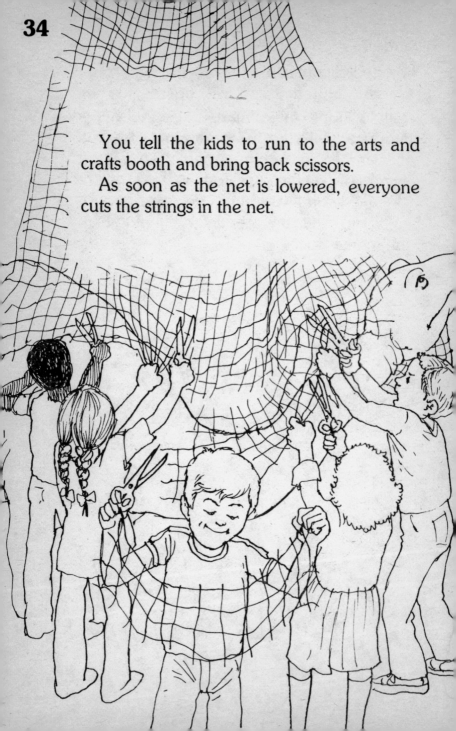

The helicopter tries to put the net around Harvey. But the net falls apart. And the helicopter flies away.

"Hooray!" shout the children. "We've saved Harvey!"

"Oh no, we haven't," you say. "They'll be back. We'd better get Harvey under cover—fast!"

If you hide Harvey in the recreation room, turn to page 38.

If you take Harvey to the sandbox and cover him with sand, turn to page 40.

"Quick!" you shout to
the children. "Climb all over
Harvey! The pilot certainly
won't drop the net over *us*."

When the pilot sees you
and your friends, he raises his
net and flies away.

"What are we going to do now?" says one of the children.

"I don't know," says another. "But if they take Harvey away, I'm going with him!"

"Me too!" shout the other children. "Wherever Harvey goes, we go!"

Turn to page 52.

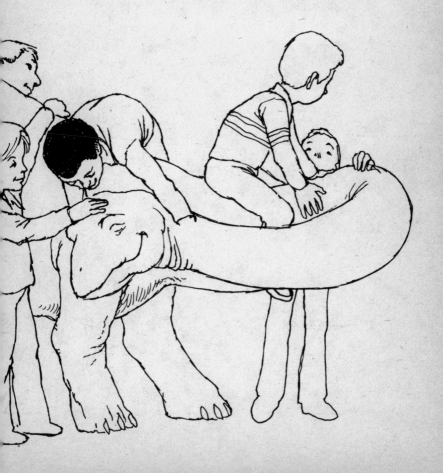

You lead Harvey to the recreation room and shove him through the door.

Before you go home for dinner, you leave Harvey a huge pile of food.

When you come back in the morning, there is a gigantic hole where the recreation room door used to be.

Harvey has escaped!

You and the other children look all over town. But you cannot find Harvey.

Night after night you listen to the evening news. Every once in a while you hear a report of a pink dinosaur wandering somewhere in the United States. You follow his progress on the map. He seems to be heading south toward the jungles.

Then, just about the time he reaches Central America, all reports of Harvey stop.

You are sure he has found his way home at last. And that makes you very happy.

The End

You and the children lead Harvey to the sandbox. Then everybody covers him up. You even make a sand castle on top of him.

But you are very careful not to cover Harvey's head.

The next time the helicopter comes, it flies right by.

All day long you play with Harvey. Every time you hear a helicopter, you cover him up with sand. Nobody except you and your friends knows where Harvey is.

But soon it is time to go home. Harvey loves the park so much that he refuses to leave.

You are afraid that he will be captured during the night.

If you try to put Harvey on wheels and roll him home, turn to page 42.

If you disguise Harvey as a tree, turn to page 44.

If you decide that Harvey really belongs in the zoo, turn to page 54.

You go to the park maintenance man and borrow two dollies. Dollies are platforms on wheels that are used for carrying heavy things.

You put Harvey on the dollies. You cover him with a huge sheet and roll him home.

Then you put Harvey in your garage.

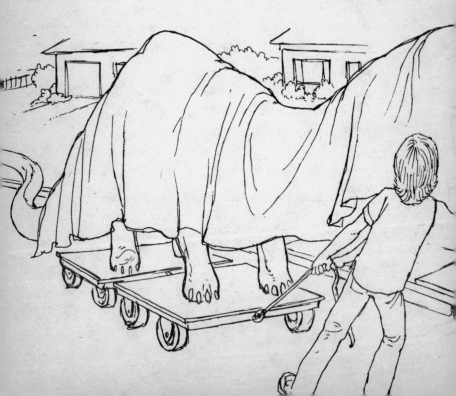

The problem is that Harvey is just a baby. Every day he grows and grows and GROWS.

In a few weeks, you move Harvey to an empty barn outside of town.

None of the adults knows where Harvey is. But children go to the barn every day and play with Harvey. There is enough of him for everybody. He is the biggest secret in town.

The End

All the kids gather branches and tie them onto Harvey. Then everyone goes home for the night.

When you arrive in the park in the morning, Harvey is not there.

You listen on the radio for news reports. But nobody has seen Harvey.

You are sad that he is gone. You miss your friend. But it makes you giggle to think that a pink dinosaur, decorated like a tree, is wandering around just waiting to surprise someone else.

The End

Luckily, one of the kids is eating a hamburger. You ask if you can use it to tempt Harvey.

You take the hamburger and wave it under Harvey's nose. Just as he reaches out for a bite, you jerk it away.

Harvey comes out of the pool fast! He wants that hamburger!

He starts to chase you. The lifeguard, the policemen, and all the children chase Harvey.

Down the street you run. *I better get him some more hamburgers,* you think. So you head straight for McDonald's.

You dash through the door. But poor Harvey gets stuck. Half of him is inside the building and half of him is outside.

You feed him the hamburger. He eats the pickles and lettuce and onions and the sesame seed bun. But he does not eat the meat because Harvey is a vegetarian.

The manager says Harvey can stay in the door as long as he wants because he is great for business.

If you want to know how the customers get in and out of the building, turn to page 50.

You call an emergency meeting of all the people in town. You ask everyone to give money to the Harvey Fund.

"What will you do with the money?" someone asks.

"We will send Harvey to Scotland. Then we will take him to the lake called Loch Ness."

"Why should he go to Loch Ness?" someone asks.

"Because that is where the Loch Ness Monster lives. And a lot of people think that the Loch Ness Monster is a dinosaur, too. That way, Harvey will have company."

"That's a great idea," everyone shouts.

And that is exactly what you do.

The End

The End

And so, when Harvey leaves the park, all the children follow him. They refuse to go home.

"Looks to me like those children mean business," says one of the parents.

"Yes," says another. "It's because they love Harvey so much."

"Well, it seems to me," says the mayor, "that if the children love the dinosaur so much, we ought to build a park just for him. A great big park, with lots of room to roam."

That is just what happens. And, to this day, if you happen to find that very town, you can still see Harvey roaming around in his enormous home. He's just the same as before . . . only much, much BIGGER.

The End

"I guess the only thing to do is to let Harvey live in the zoo," someone says.

"But we won't tell the zoo people where Harvey is," you say, "until they promise to build him a gigantic home. After all, this brontosaurus needs a lot of space."

The zoo people build Harvey a mansion. They move Harvey on a huge flatbed truck to his new home.

Every day you visit Harvey. He is very happy.

He makes lots and lots of friends. And he gets tons of food to eat every day.

If you want to know who Harvey's best friends are, turn the page.

The End